STAR WARS ADVENTURES

6

ROSE KNOWS

Writer: Delilah S. Dawson
Artist: Derek Charm
Letterer: Tom B. Long

TALES FROM WILD SPACE
"PODRACER'S RESCUE"

SEE PAGE 17

Writer: Shaun Manning
Artist: Chad Thomas
Colorist: Charlie Kirchoff
Letterer: Tom B. Long

ABDO · Spotlight · IDW · Disney · LUCASFILM

ABDOBOOKS.COM

Reinforced library bound edition published in 2019 by Spotlight, a division of ABDO,
PO Box 398166, Minneapolis, Minnesota 55439. Spotlight produces high-quality
reinforced library bound editions for schools and libraries.
Published by agreement with IDW.

Printed in the United States of America, North Mankato, Minnesota.
092018
012019

THIS BOOK CONTAINS
RECYCLED MATERIALS

Library of Congress Control Number: 2018945157

Publisher's Cataloging-in-Publication Data

Names: Dawson, Delilah S.; Manning, Shaun, authors. | Charm, Derek; Thomas, Chad;
    Kirchoff, Charlie, illustrators.
Title: Star Wars adventures #6: Rose knows / by Delilah S. Dawson and Shaun Manning ;
    illustrated by Derek Charm, Chad Thomas, and Charlie Kirchoff.
Description: Minneapolis, Minnesota : Spotlight, 2019. | Series: Star Wars adventures
Summary: It's up to Rose to figure out how to open the jammed hangar bay doors during an
    Imperial attack, and a young Anakin Skywalker has found a power cell he needs for his
    podracer but learns someone else might need it more than he does.
Identifiers: ISBN 9781532142901 (lib. bdg.)
Subjects: LCSH: Star Wars fiction--Juvenile fiction. | Space warfare--Juvenile fiction. |
    Extraterrestrial beings--Juvenile fiction. | Good and evil--Juvenile fiction. | Heroes--
    Juvenile fiction.
Classification: DDC 741.5--dc23

Spotlight

A Division of ABDO
abdobooks.com

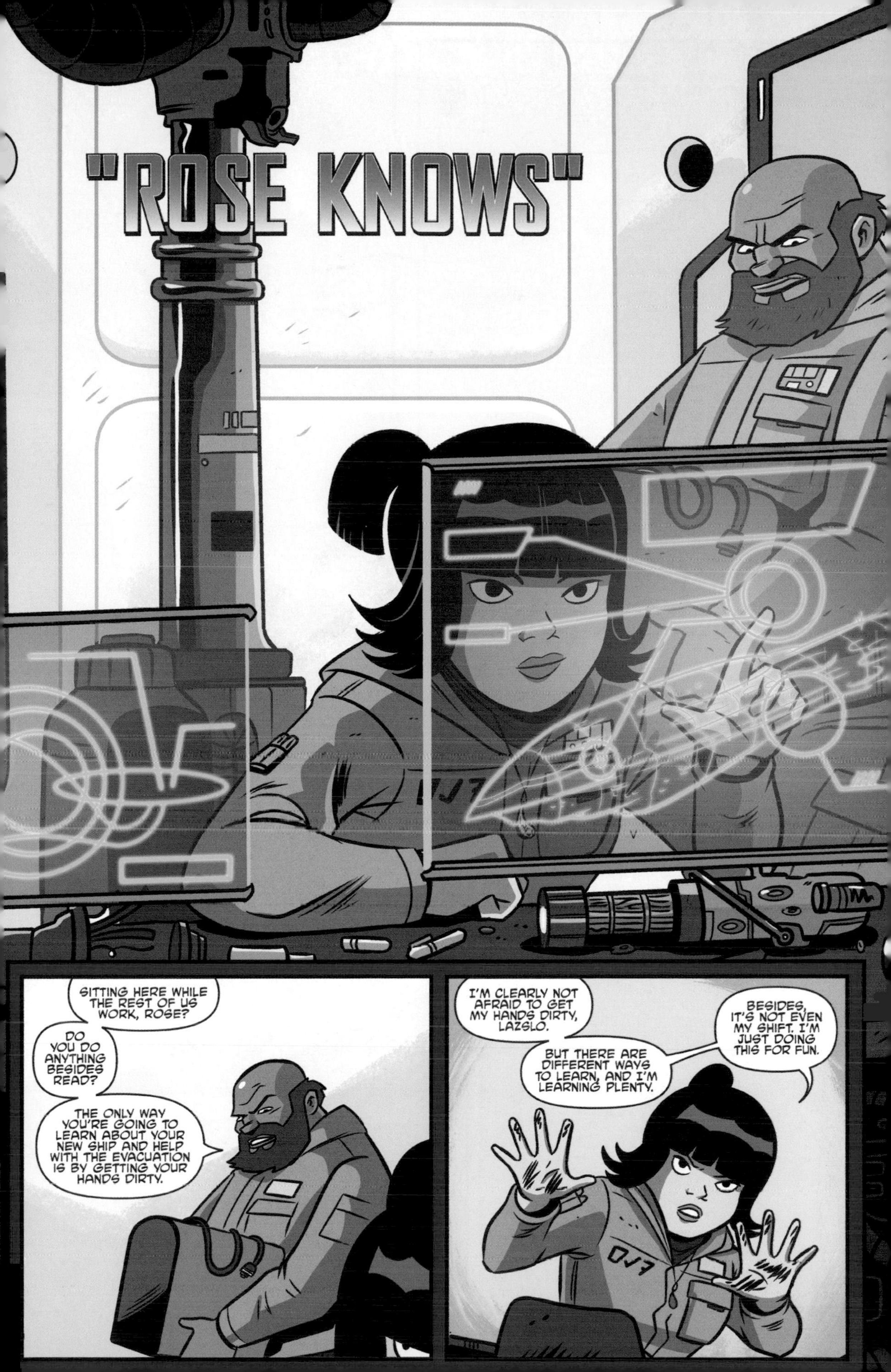
"ROSE KNOWS"
SITTING HERE WHILE THE REST OF US WORK, ROSE?
DO YOU DO ANYTHING BESIDES READ?
THE ONLY WAY YOU'RE GOING TO LEARN ABOUT YOUR NEW SHIP AND HELP WITH THE EVACUATION IS BY GETTING YOUR HANDS DIRTY.
I'M CLEARLY NOT AFRAID TO GET MY HANDS DIRTY, LAZSLO.
BUT THERE ARE DIFFERENT WAYS TO LEARN, AND I'M LEARNING PLENTY.
BESIDES, IT'S NOT EVEN MY SHIFT. I'M JUST DOING THIS FOR FUN.

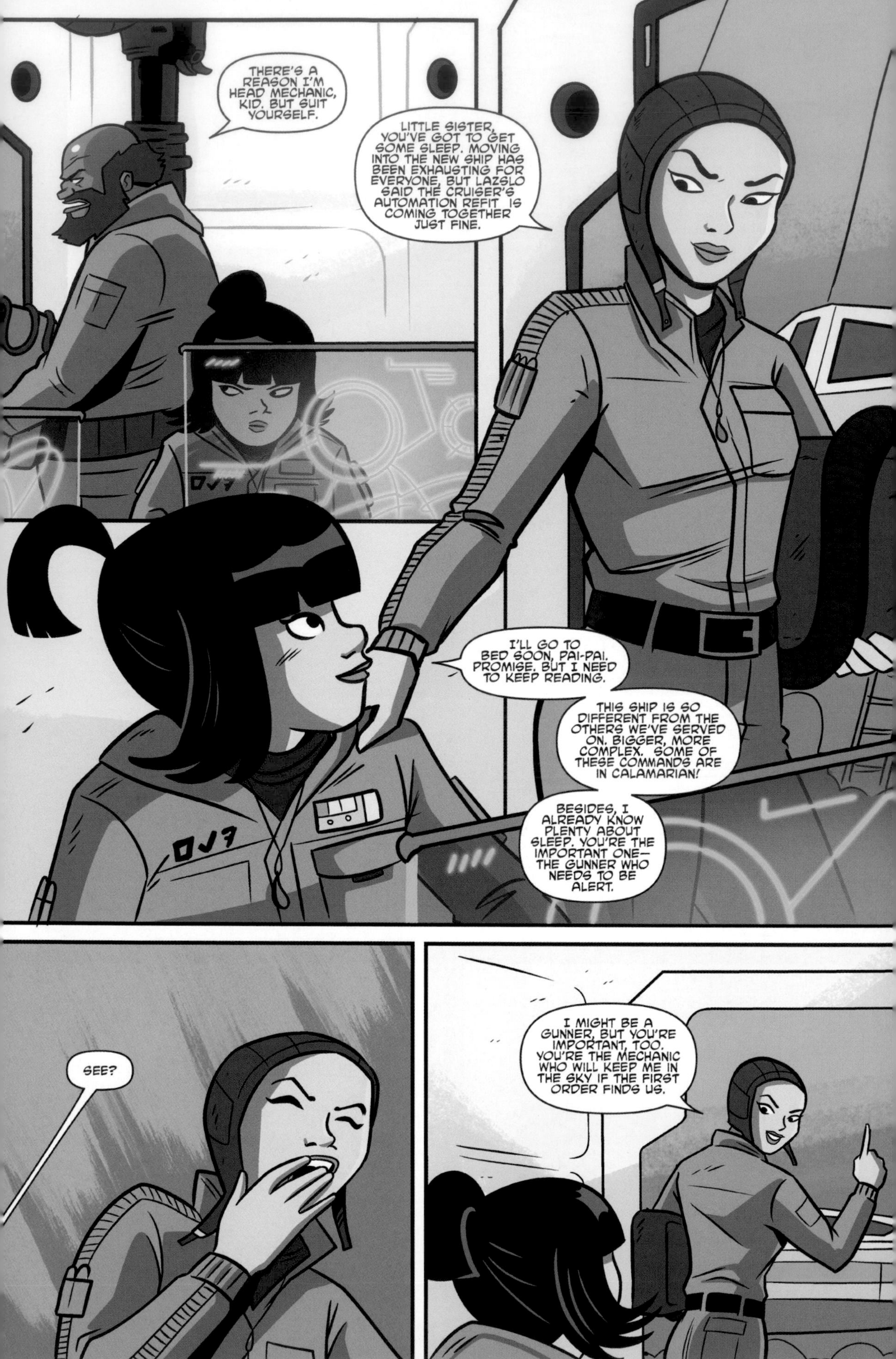
THERE'S A REASON I'M HEAD MECHANIC, KID. BUT SUIT YOURSELF.
LITTLE SISTER, YOU'VE GOT TO GET SOME SLEEP. MOVING INTO THE NEW SHIP HAS BEEN EXHAUSTING FOR EVERYONE, BUT LAZSLO SAID THE CRUISER'S AUTOMATION REFIT IS COMING TOGETHER JUST FINE.
I'LL GO TO BED SOON, PAI-PAI. PROMISE. BUT I NEED TO KEEP READING.
THIS SHIP IS SO DIFFERENT FROM THE OTHERS WE'VE SERVED ON. BIGGER, MORE COMPLEX. SOME OF THESE COMMANDS ARE IN CALAMARIAN!
BESIDES, I ALREADY KNOW PLENTY ABOUT SLEEP. YOU'RE THE IMPORTANT ONE— THE GUNNER WHO NEEDS TO BE ALERT.
SEE?
I MIGHT BE A GUNNER, BUT YOU'RE IMPORTANT, TOO. YOU'RE THE MECHANIC WHO WILL KEEP ME IN THE SKY IF THE FIRST ORDER FINDS US.

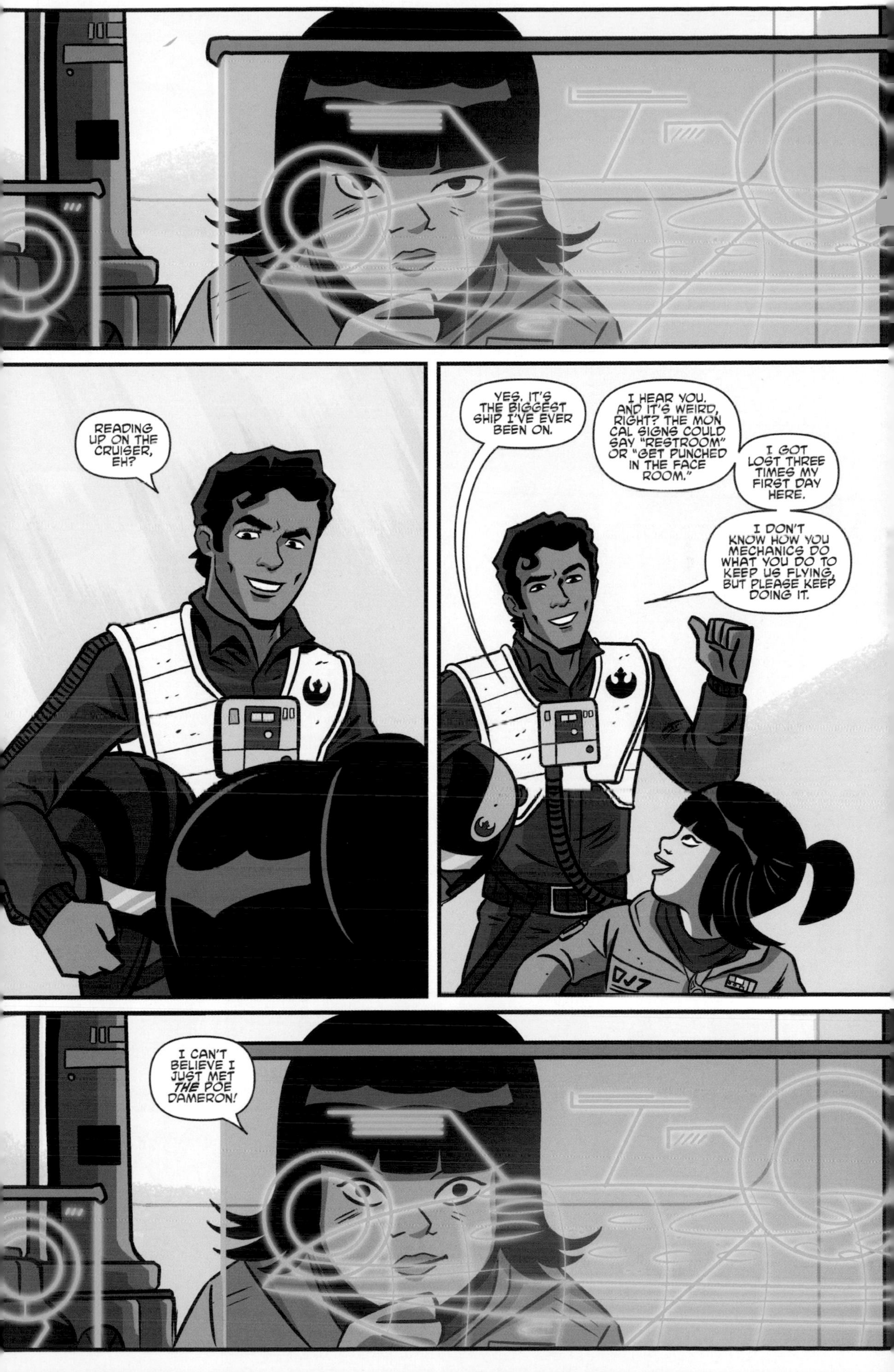

READING UP ON THE CRUISER, EH?
YES. IT'S THE BIGGEST SHIP I'VE EVER BEEN ON.
I HEAR YOU. AND IT'S WEIRD, RIGHT? THE MON CAL SIGNS COULD SAY "RESTROOM" OR "GET PUNCHED IN THE FACE ROOM."
I GOT LOST THREE TIMES MY FIRST DAY HERE.
I DON'T KNOW HOW YOU MECHANICS DO WHAT YOU DO TO KEEP US FLYING, BUT PLEASE KEEP DOING IT.
I CAN'T BELIEVE I JUST MET *THE* POE DAMERON!

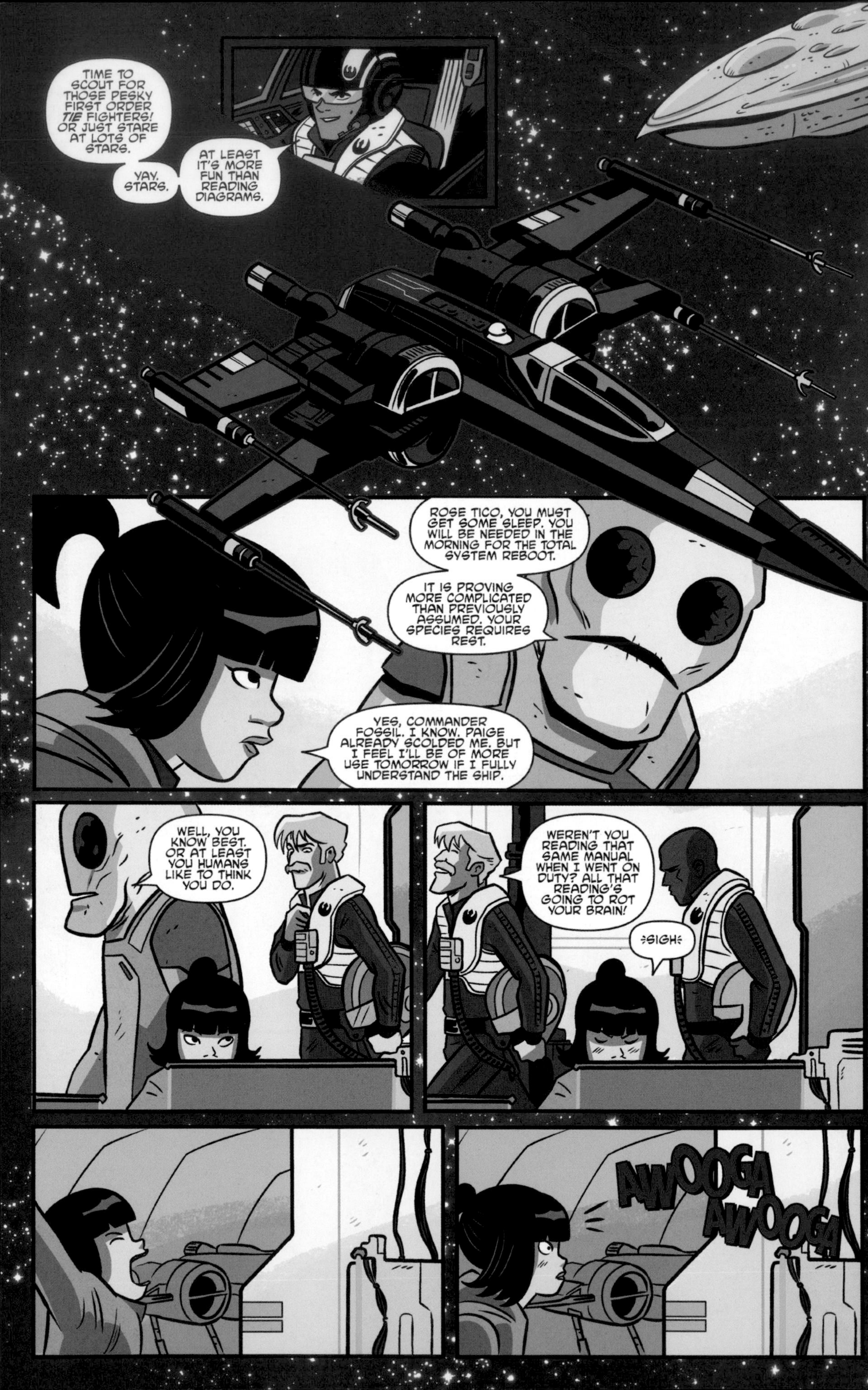
TIME TO SCOUT FOR THOSE PESKY FIRST ORDER TIE FIGHTERS! OR JUST STARE AT LOTS OF STARS.
YAY. STARS.
AT LEAST IT'S MORE FUN THAN READING DIAGRAMS.
ROSE TICO, YOU MUST GET SOME SLEEP. YOU WILL BE NEEDED IN THE MORNING FOR THE TOTAL SYSTEM REBOOT.
IT IS PROVING MORE COMPLICATED THAN PREVIOUSLY ASSUMED. YOUR SPECIES REQUIRES REST.
YES, COMMANDER FOSSIL. I KNOW. PAIGE ALREADY SCOLDED ME. BUT I FEEL I'LL BE OF MORE USE TOMORROW IF I FULLY UNDERSTAND THE SHIP.
WELL, YOU KNOW BEST. OR AT LEAST YOU HUMANS LIKE TO THINK YOU DO.
WEREN'T YOU READING THAT SAME MANUAL WHEN I WENT ON DUTY? ALL THAT READING'S GOING TO ROT YOUR BRAIN!
SIGH
AWOOGA AWOOGA

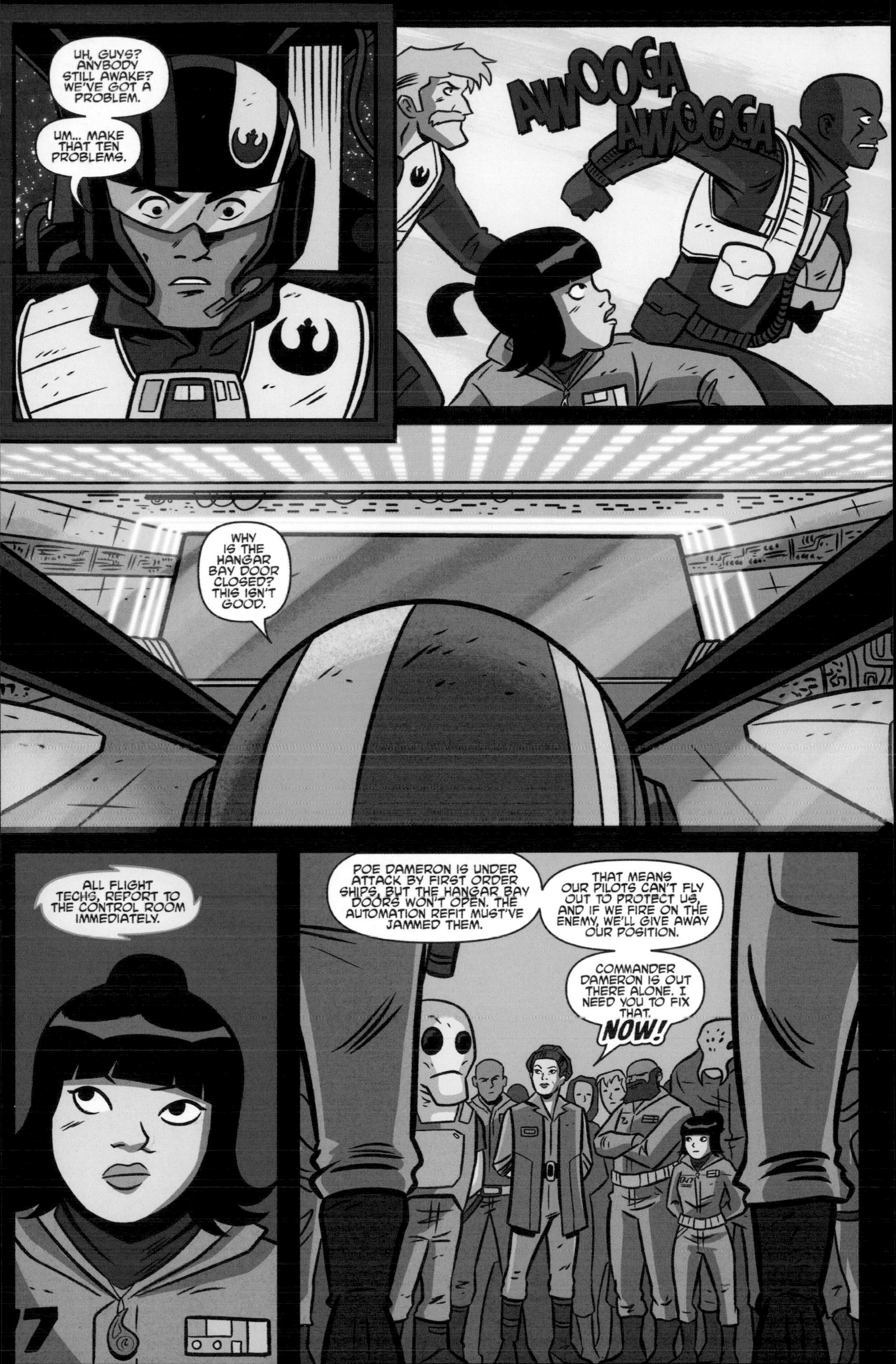
UH, GUYS? ANYBODY STILL AWAKE? WE'VE GOT A PROBLEM.
UM... MAKE THAT TEN PROBLEMS.
AWOOGA
AWOOGA
WHY IS THE HANGAR BAY DOOR CLOSED? THIS ISN'T GOOD.
ALL FLIGHT TECHS, REPORT TO THE CONTROL ROOM IMMEDIATELY.
POE DAMERON IS UNDER ATTACK BY FIRST ORDER SHIPS, BUT THE HANGAR BAY DOORS WON'T OPEN. THE AUTOMATION REFIT MUST'VE JAMMED THEM.
THAT MEANS OUR PILOTS CAN'T FLY OUT TO PROTECT US, AND IF WE FIRE ON THE ENEMY, WE'LL GIVE AWAY OUR POSITION.
COMMANDER DAMERON IS OUT THERE ALONE. I NEED YOU TO FIX THAT. NOW!

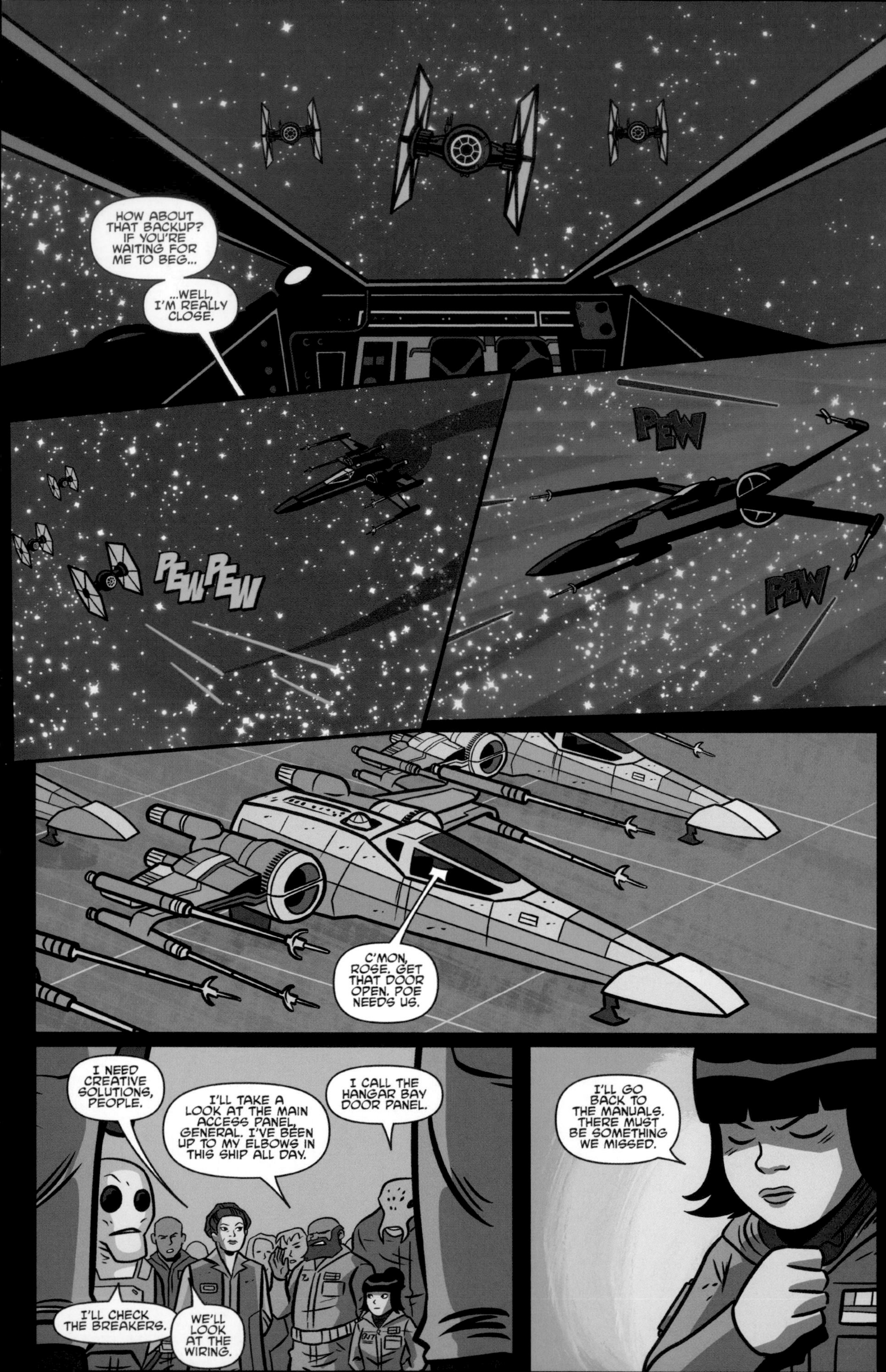

HOW ABOUT THAT BACKUP? IF YOU'RE WAITING FOR ME TO BEG...
...WELL, I'M REALLY CLOSE.
PEW PEW
PEW
PEW
C'MON, ROSE. GET THAT DOOR OPEN. POE NEEDS US.
I NEED CREATIVE SOLUTIONS, PEOPLE.
I'LL TAKE A LOOK AT THE MAIN ACCESS PANEL, GENERAL. I'VE BEEN UP TO MY ELBOWS IN THIS SHIP ALL DAY.
I CALL THE HANGAR BAY DOOR PANEL.
I'LL CHECK THE BREAKERS.
WE'LL LOOK AT THE WIRING.
I'LL GO BACK TO THE MANUALS. THERE MUST BE SOMETHING WE MISSED.

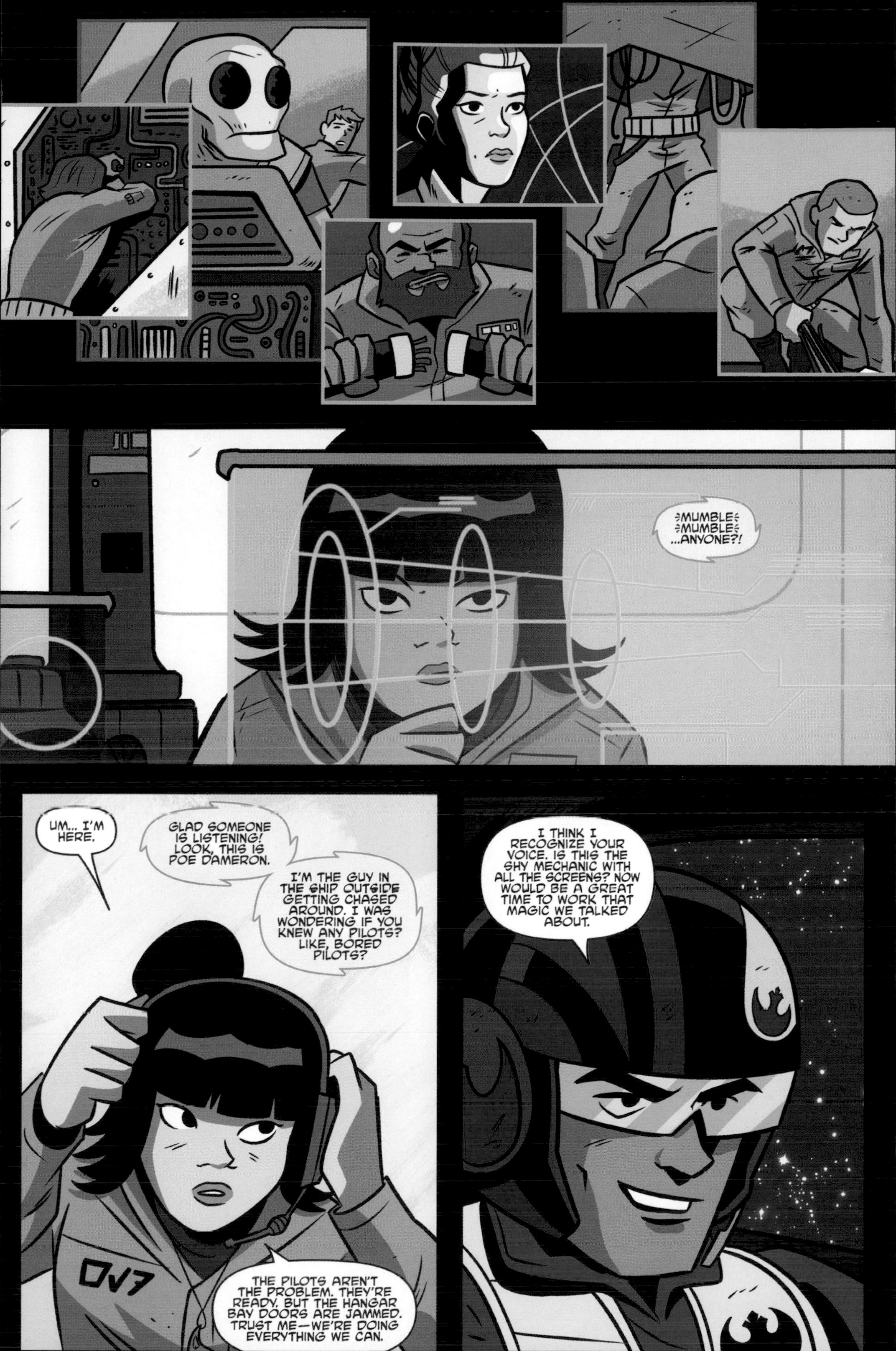

MUMBLE *MUMBLE* ...ANYONE?!
UM... I'M HERE.
GLAD SOMEONE IS LISTENING! LOOK, THIS IS POE DAMERON.
I'M THE GUY IN THE SHIP OUTSIDE GETTING CHASED AROUND. I WAS WONDERING IF YOU KNEW ANY PILOTS? LIKE, BORED PILOTS?
DV7
THE PILOTS AREN'T THE PROBLEM. THEY'RE READY. BUT THE HANGAR BAY DOORS ARE JAMMED. TRUST ME—WE'RE DOING EVERYTHING WE CAN.
I THINK I RECOGNIZE YOUR VOICE. IS THIS THE SHY MECHANIC WITH ALL THE SCREENS? NOW WOULD BE A GREAT TIME TO WORK THAT MAGIC WE TALKED ABOUT.

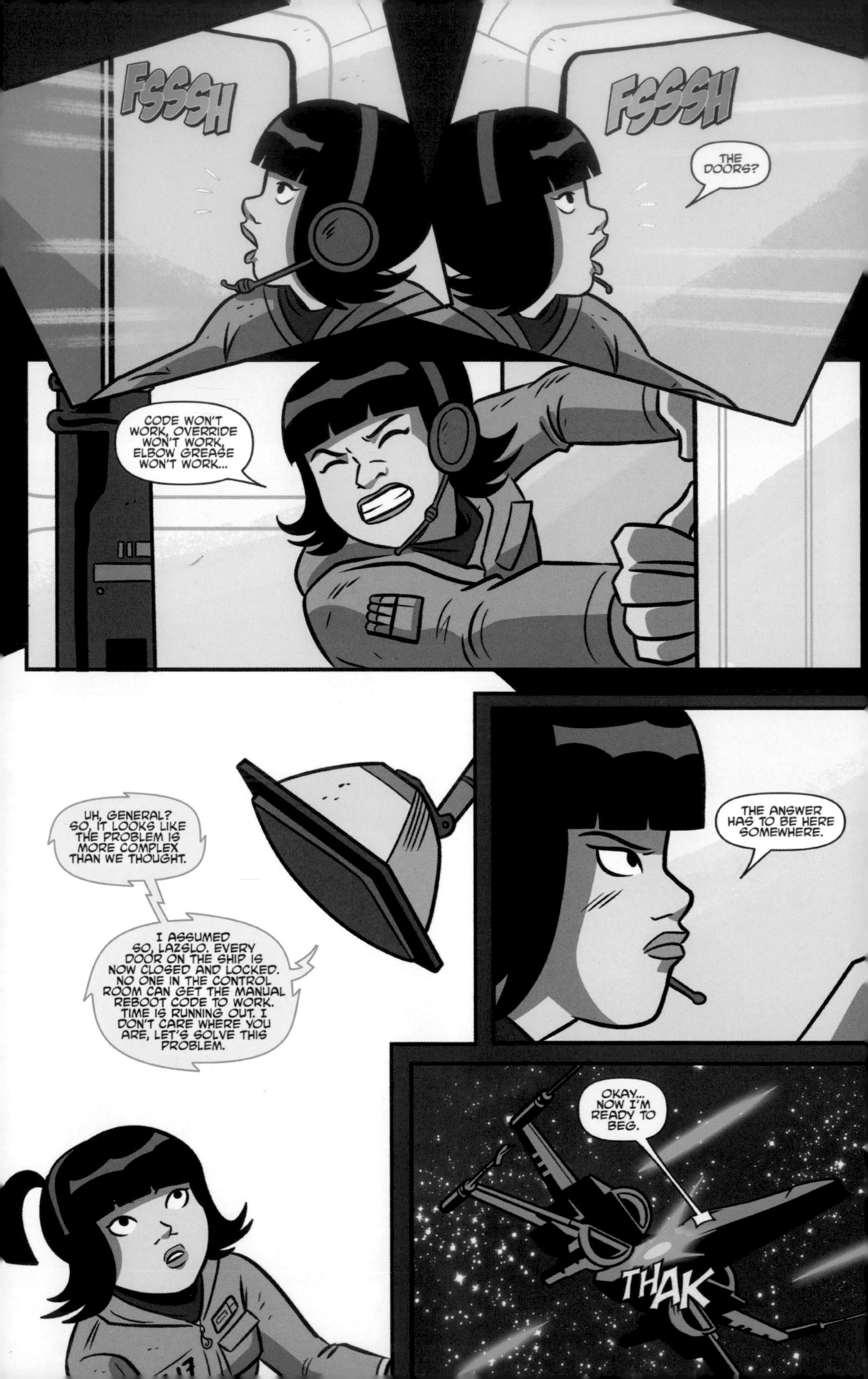
FSSSH
FSSSH
THE DOORS?
CODE WON'T WORK, OVERRIDE WON'T WORK, ELBOW GREASE WON'T WORK...
THE ANSWER HAS TO BE HERE SOMEWHERE.
UH, GENERAL? SO, IT LOOKS LIKE THE PROBLEM IS MORE COMPLEX THAN WE THOUGHT.
I ASSUMED SO, LAZSLO. EVERY DOOR ON THE SHIP IS NOW CLOSED AND LOCKED. NO ONE IN THE CONTROL ROOM CAN GET THE MANUAL REBOOT CODE TO WORK. TIME IS RUNNING OUT. I DON'T CARE WHERE YOU ARE, LET'S SOLVE THIS PROBLEM.
OKAY... NOW I'M READY TO BEG.
THAK

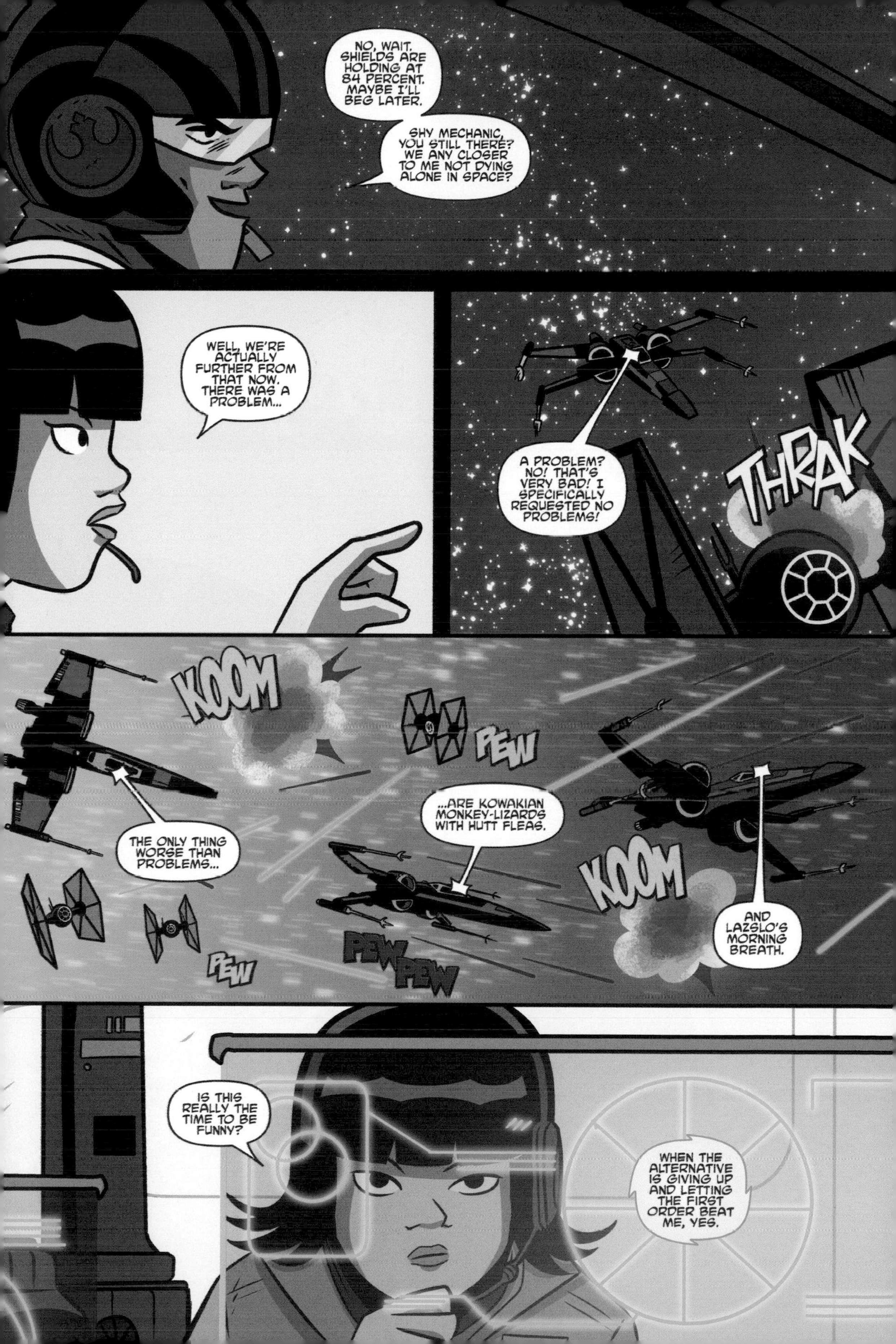
NO, WAIT. SHIELDS ARE HOLDING AT 84 PERCENT. MAYBE I'LL BEG LATER.
SHY MECHANIC, YOU STILL THERE? WE ANY CLOSER TO ME NOT DYING ALONE IN SPACE?
WELL, WE'RE ACTUALLY FURTHER FROM THAT NOW. THERE WAS A PROBLEM...
A PROBLEM? NO! THAT'S VERY BAD! I SPECIFICALLY REQUESTED NO PROBLEMS!
THRAK
KOOM
PEW
THE ONLY THING WORSE THAN PROBLEMS...
...ARE KOWAKIAN MONKEY-LIZARDS WITH HUTT FLEAS.
KOOM
AND LAZSLO'S MORNING BREATH.
PEW
PEW PEW
IS THIS REALLY THE TIME TO BE FUNNY?
WHEN THE ALTERNATIVE IS GIVING UP AND LETTING THE FIRST ORDER BEAT ME, YES.

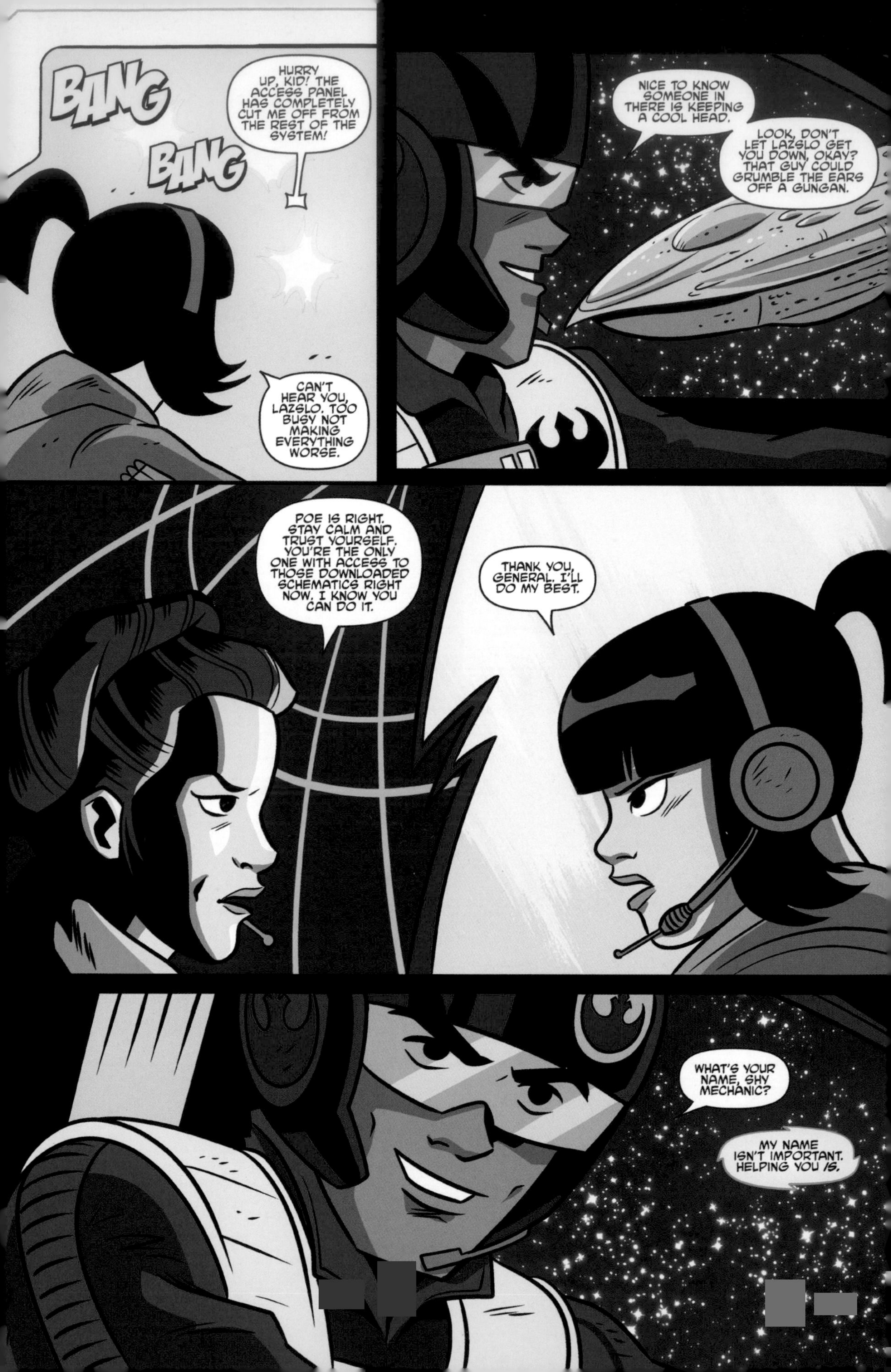
BANG
BANG
HURRY UP, KID! THE ACCESS PANEL HAS COMPLETELY CUT ME OFF FROM THE REST OF THE SYSTEM!
CAN'T HEAR YOU, LAZSLO. TOO BUSY NOT MAKING EVERYTHING WORSE.
NICE TO KNOW SOMEONE IN THERE IS KEEPING A COOL HEAD.
LOOK, DON'T LET LAZSLO GET YOU DOWN, OKAY? THAT GUY COULD GRUMBLE THE EARS OFF A GUNGAN.
POE IS RIGHT. STAY CALM AND TRUST YOURSELF. YOU'RE THE ONLY ONE WITH ACCESS TO THOSE DOWNLOADED SCHEMATICS RIGHT NOW. I KNOW YOU CAN DO IT.
THANK YOU, GENERAL. I'LL DO MY BEST.
WHAT'S YOUR NAME, SHY MECHANIC?
MY NAME ISN'T IMPORTANT. HELPING YOU IS.

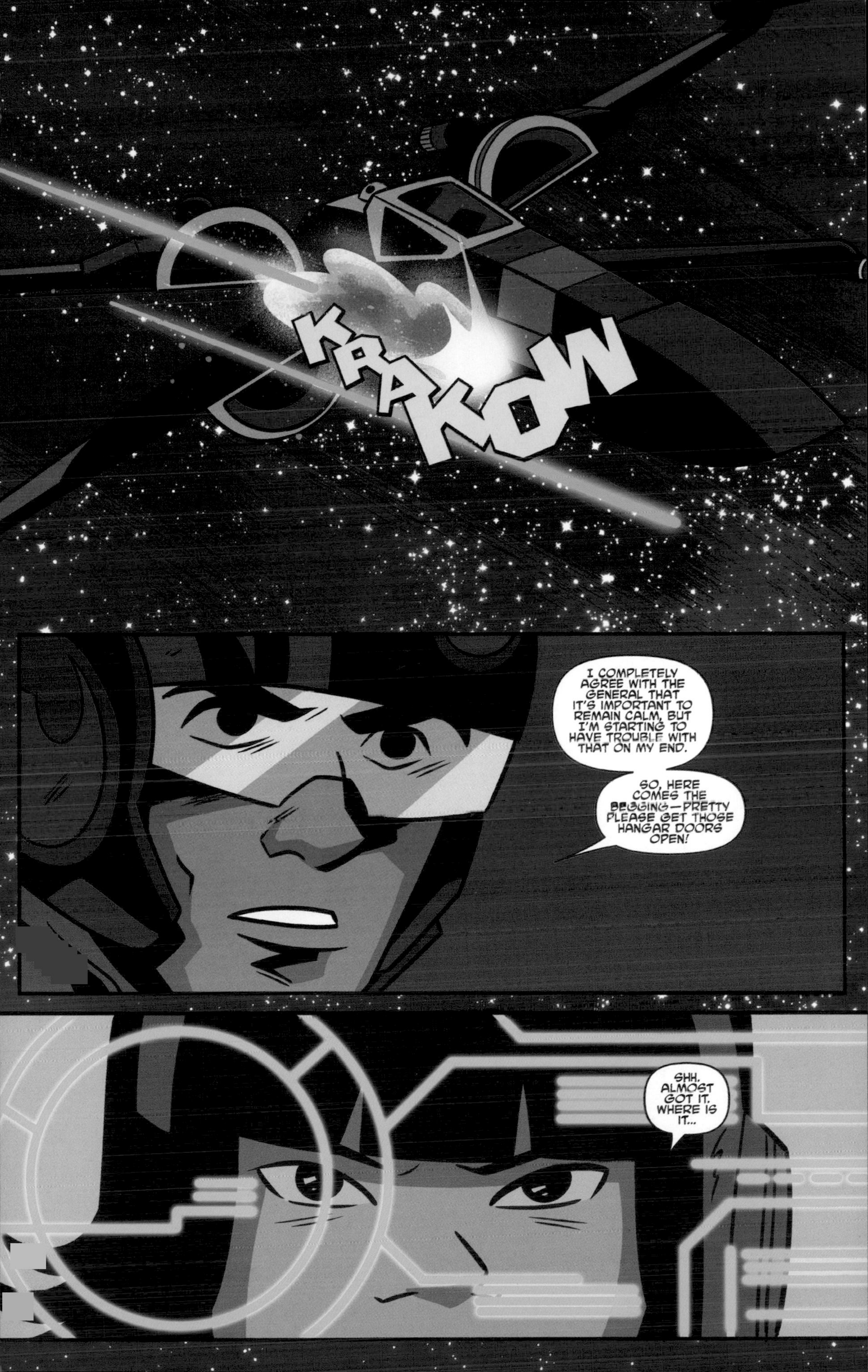
KRAKOW
I COMPLETELY AGREE WITH THE GENERAL THAT IT'S IMPORTANT TO REMAIN CALM, BUT I'M STARTING TO HAVE TROUBLE WITH THAT ON MY END.
SO, HERE COMES THE BEGGING—PRETTY PLEASE GET THOSE HANGAR DOORS OPEN!
SHH. ALMOST GOT IT. WHERE IS IT...

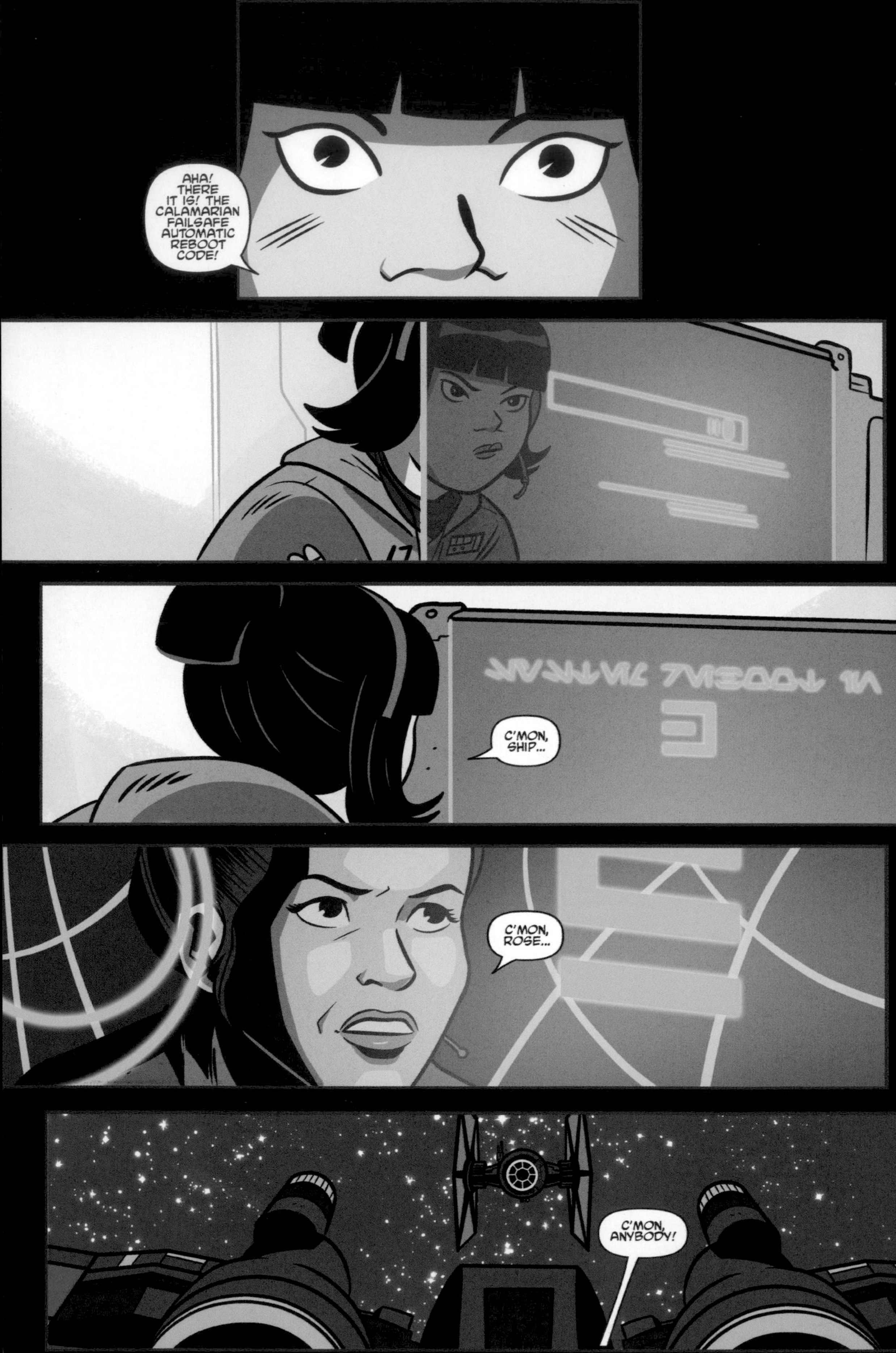
AHA! THERE IT IS! THE CALAMARIAN FAILSAFE AUTOMATIC REBOOT CODE!
C'MON, SHIP...
C'MON, ROSE...
C'MON, ANYBODY!

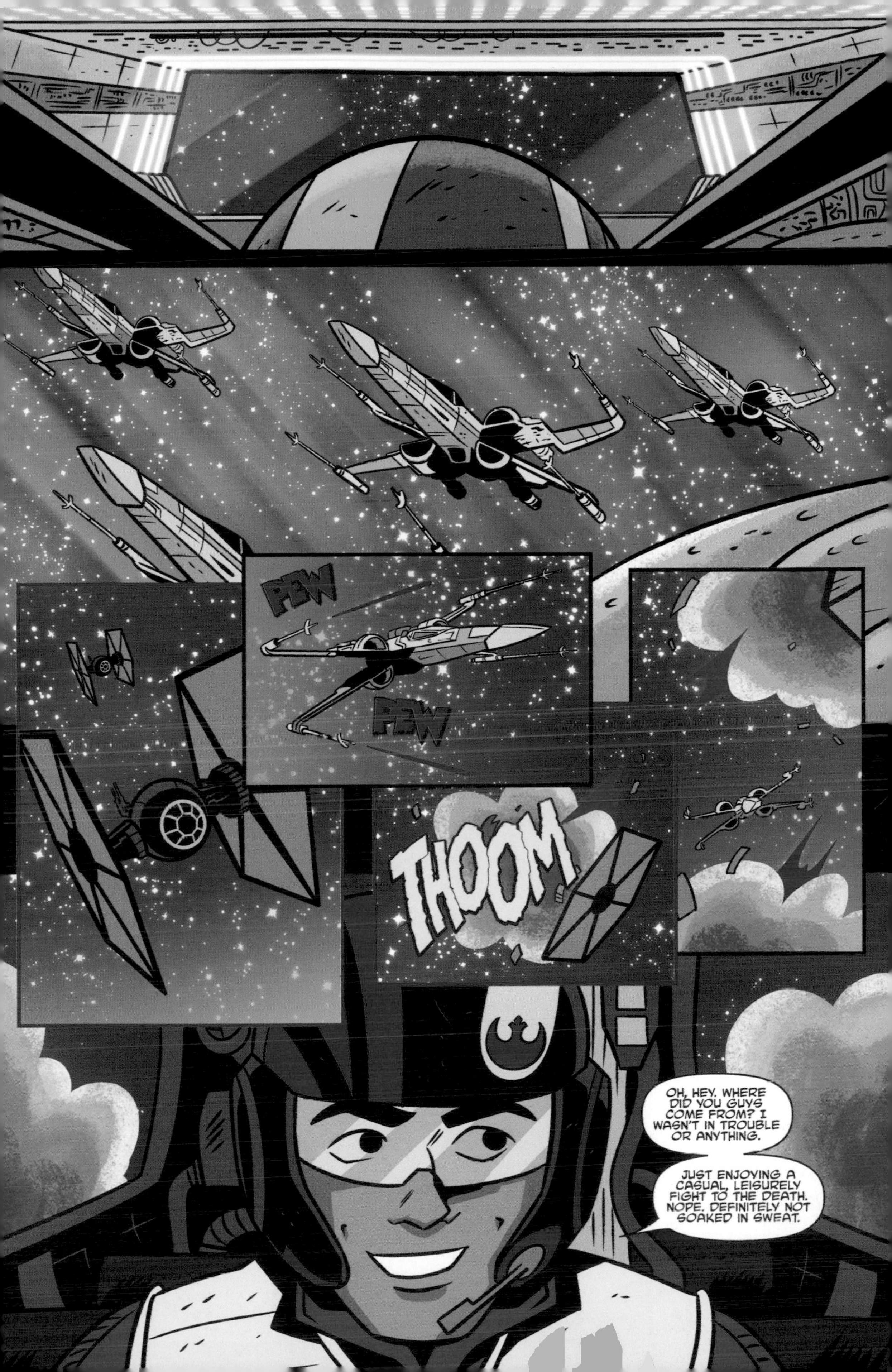
PEW
PEW
THOOM
OH, HEY. WHERE DID YOU GUYS COME FROM? I WASN'T IN TROUBLE OR ANYTHING.
JUST ENJOYING A CASUAL, LEISURELY FIGHT TO THE DEATH. NOPE. DEFINITELY NOT SOAKED IN SWEAT.

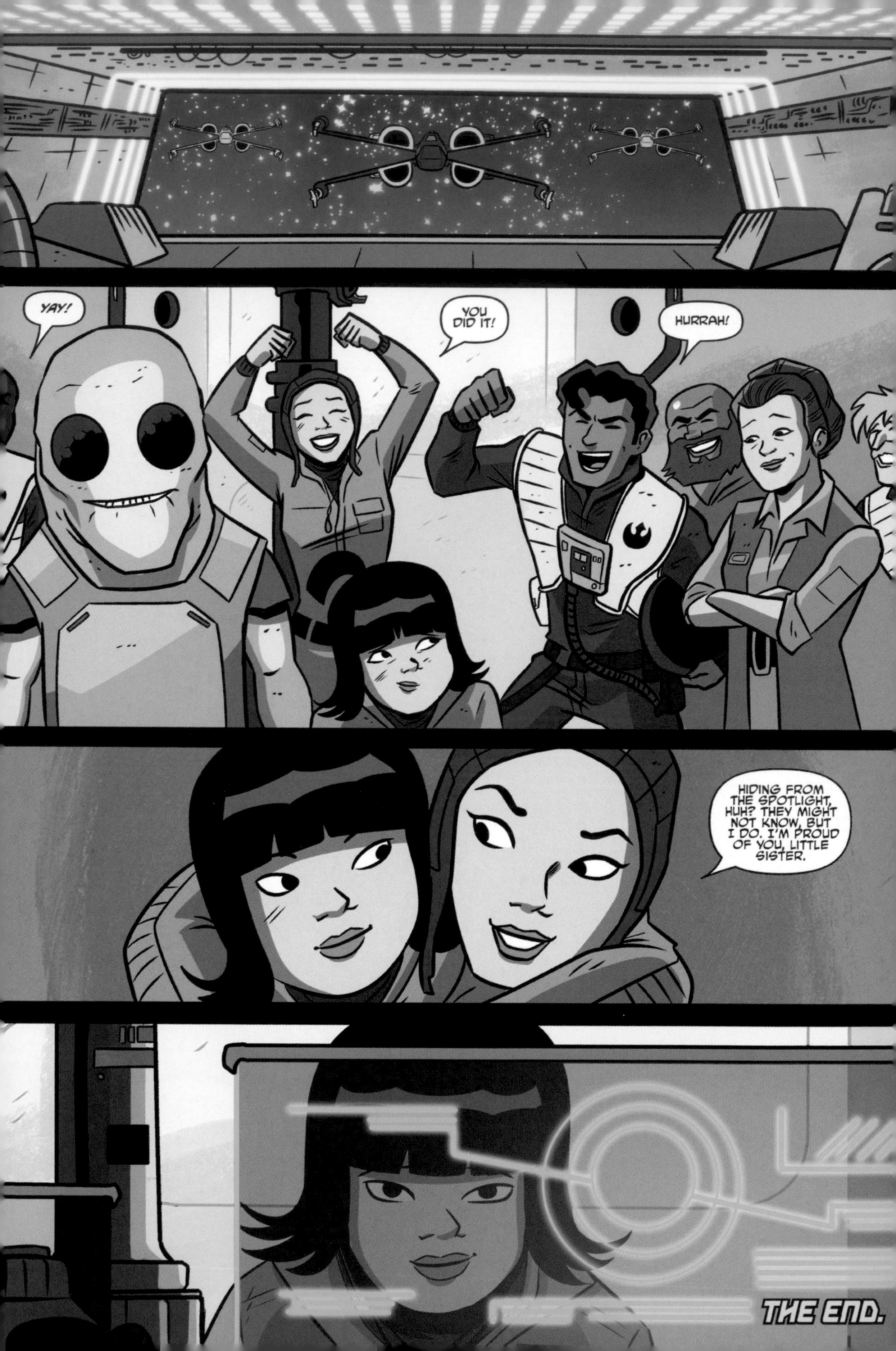
YAY!
YOU DID IT!
HURRAH!
HIDING FROM THE SPOTLIGHT, HUH? THEY MIGHT NOT KNOW, BUT I DO. I'M PROUD OF YOU, LITTLE SISTER.
THE END.

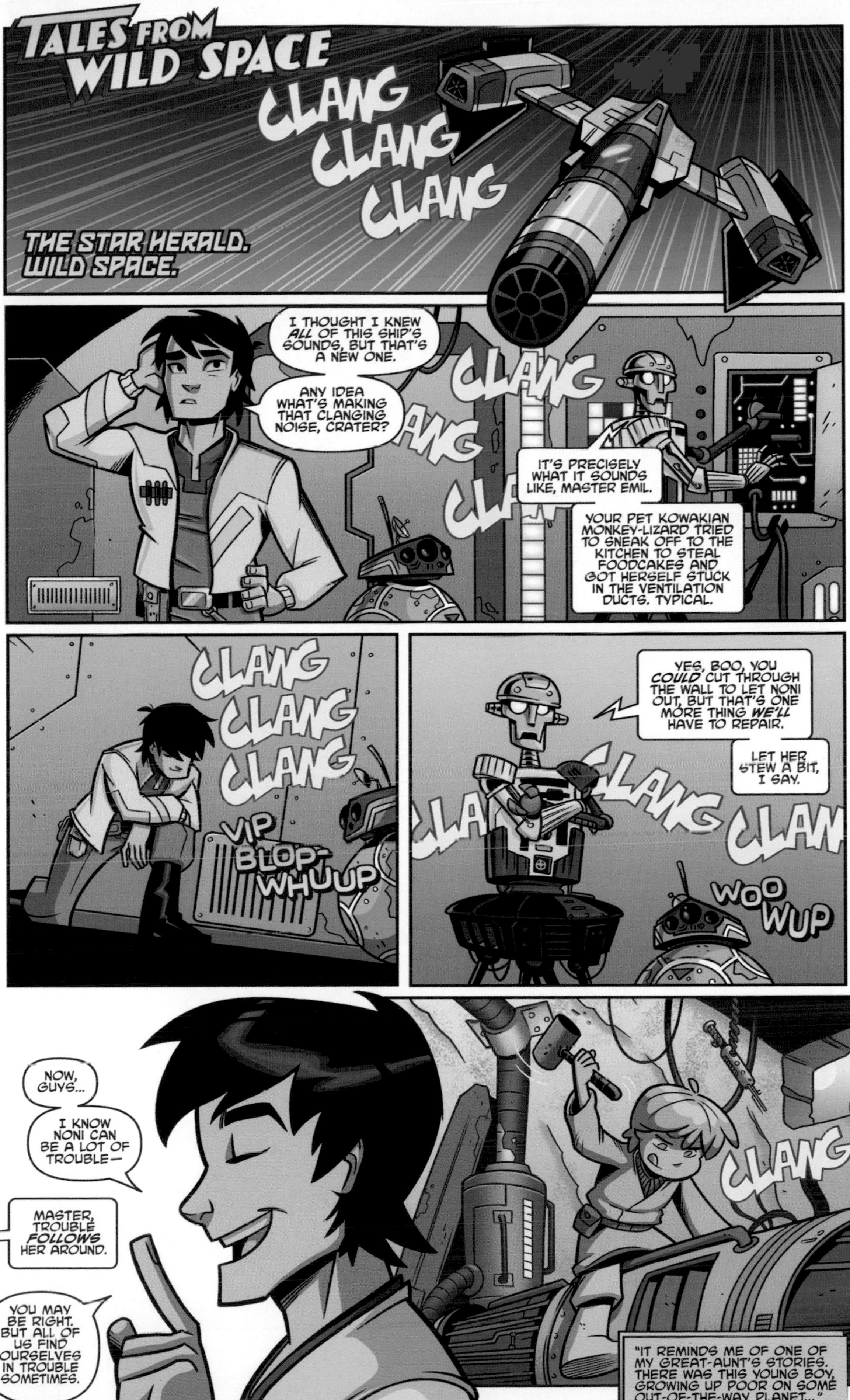
TALES FROM WILD SPACE
CLANG CLANG CLANG
THE STAR HERALD. WILD SPACE.
I THOUGHT I KNEW ALL OF THIS SHIP'S SOUNDS, BUT THAT'S A NEW ONE.
ANY IDEA WHAT'S MAKING THAT CLANGING NOISE, CRATER?
CLANG
IT'S PRECISELY WHAT IT SOUNDS LIKE, MASTER EMIL.
YOUR PET KOWAKIAN MONKEY-LIZARD TRIED TO SNEAK OFF TO THE KITCHEN TO STEAL FOODCAKES AND GOT HERSELF STUCK IN THE VENTILATION DUCTS. TYPICAL.
CLANG CLANG CLANG
VIP BLOP-WHUUP
YES, BOO, YOU COULD CUT THROUGH THE WALL TO LET NONI OUT, BUT THAT'S ONE MORE THING WE'LL HAVE TO REPAIR.
LET HER STEW A BIT, I SAY.
CLANG
WOO WUP
NOW, GUYS...
I KNOW NONI CAN BE A LOT OF TROUBLE—
MASTER, TROUBLE FOLLOWS HER AROUND.
YOU MAY BE RIGHT. BUT ALL OF US FIND OURSELVES IN TROUBLE SOMETIMES.
CLANG
"IT REMINDS ME OF ONE OF MY GREAT-AUNT'S STORIES. THERE WAS THIS YOUNG BOY, GROWING UP POOR ON SOME OUT-OF-THE-WAY PLANET..."

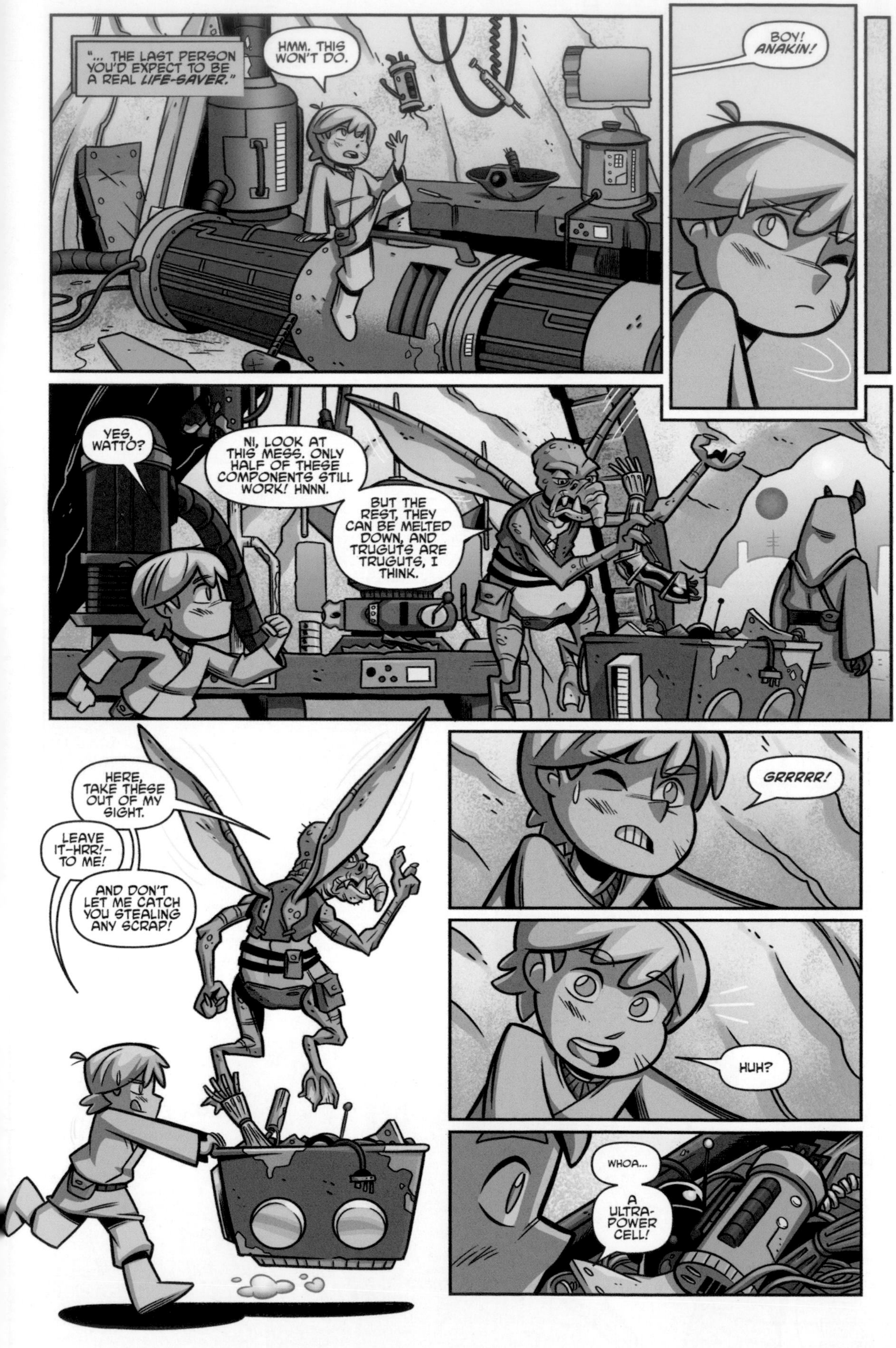
"... THE LAST PERSON YOU'D EXPECT TO BE A REAL LIFE-SAVER."
HMM. THIS WON'T DO.
BOY! ANAKIN!
YES, WATTO?
NI, LOOK AT THIS MESS. ONLY HALF OF THESE COMPONENTS STILL WORK! HNNN.
BUT THE REST, THEY CAN BE MELTED DOWN, AND TRUGUTS ARE TRUGUTS, I THINK.
HERE, TAKE THESE OUT OF MY SIGHT.
LEAVE IT–HRR!– TO ME!
AND DON'T LET ME CATCH YOU STEALING ANY SCRAP!
GRRRRR!
HUH?
WHOA...
A ULTRA-POWER CELL!

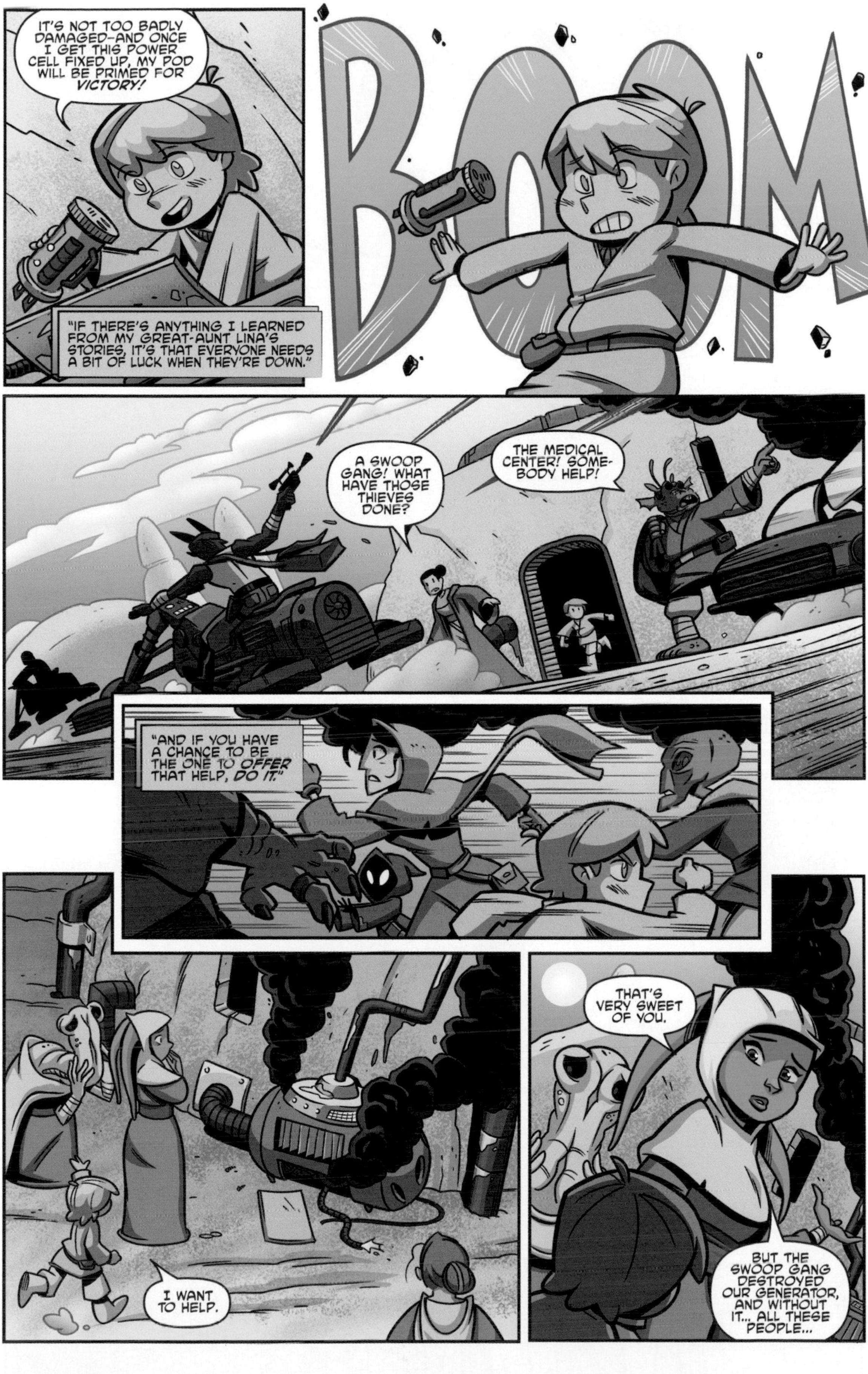

IT'S NOT TOO BADLY DAMAGED—AND ONCE I GET THIS POWER CELL FIXED UP, MY POD WILL BE PRIMED FOR *VICTORY!*
"IF THERE'S ANYTHING I LEARNED FROM MY GREAT-AUNT LINA'S STORIES, IT'S THAT EVERYONE NEEDS A BIT OF LUCK WHEN THEY'RE DOWN."
BOOM
A SWOOP GANG! WHAT HAVE THOSE THIEVES DONE?
THE MEDICAL CENTER! SOMEBODY HELP!
"AND IF YOU HAVE A CHANCE TO BE THE ONE TO *OFFER* THAT HELP, *DO IT.*"
I WANT TO HELP.
THAT'S VERY SWEET OF YOU.
BUT THE SWOOP GANG DESTROYED OUR GENERATOR, AND WITHOUT IT... ALL THESE PEOPLE...

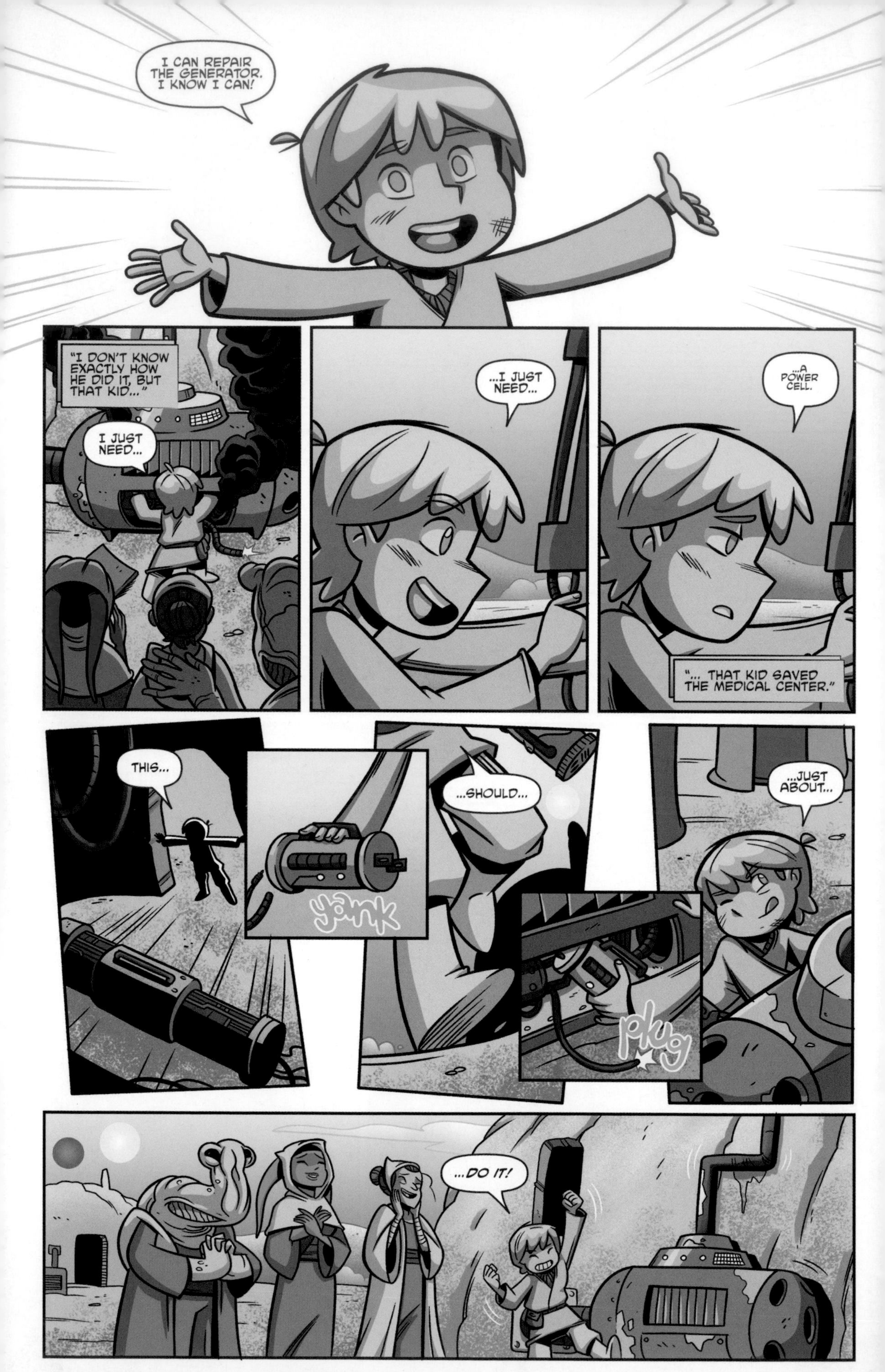
I CAN REPAIR THE GENERATOR. I KNOW I CAN!
"I DON'T KNOW EXACTLY HOW HE DID IT, BUT THAT KID..."
I JUST NEED...
...I JUST NEED...
...A POWER CELL.
"... THAT KID SAVED THE MEDICAL CENTER."
THIS...
yank
...SHOULD...
...JUST ABOUT...
plug
...DO IT!

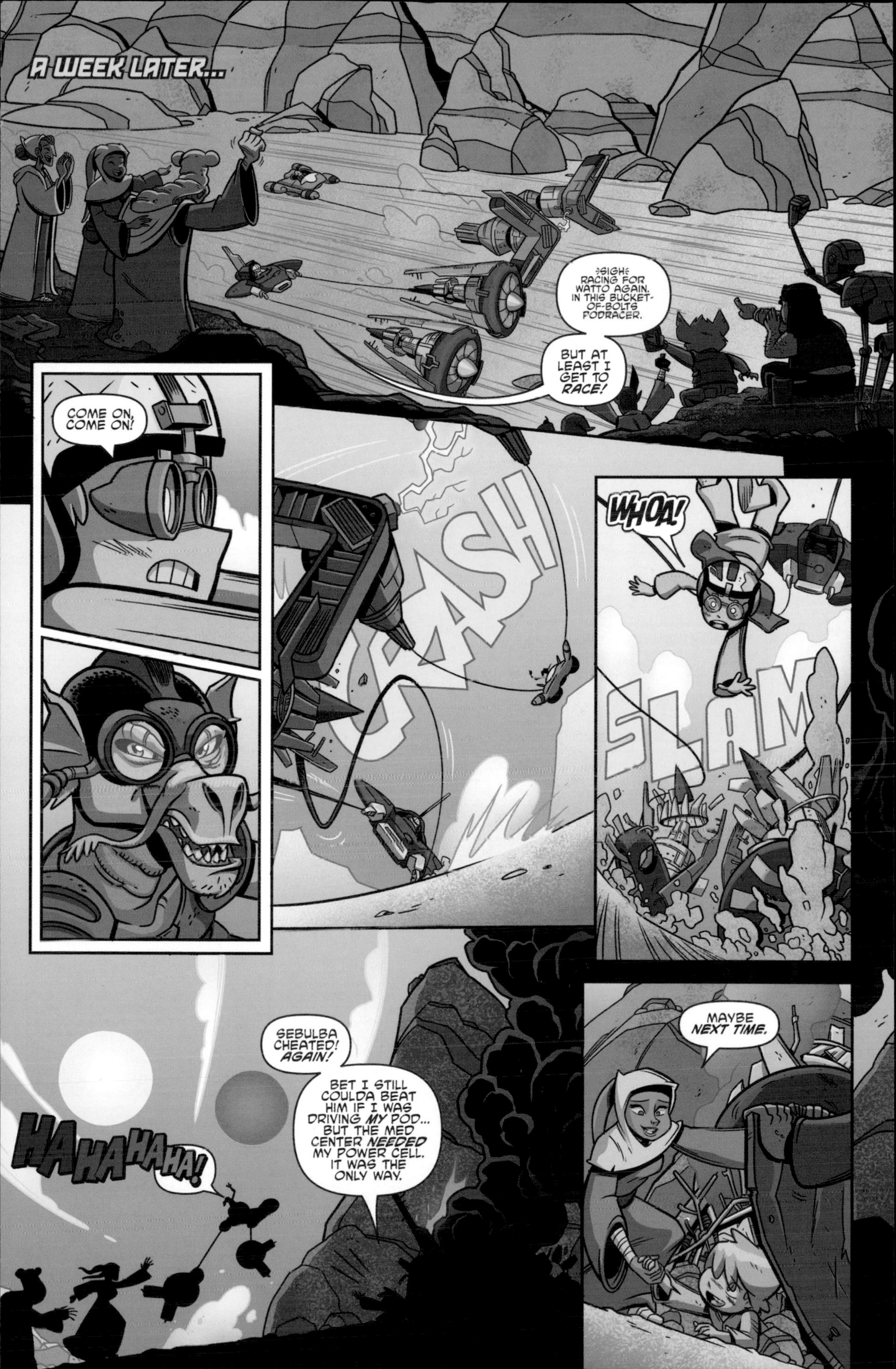
A WEEK LATER...
SIGH
RACING FOR WATTO AGAIN. IN THIS BUCKET-OF-BOLTS PODRACER.
BUT AT LEAST I GET TO RACE!
COME ON, COME ON!
CRASH
WHOA!
SLAM
SEBULBA CHEATED! AGAIN!
BET I STILL COULDA BEAT HIM IF I WAS DRIVING MY POD... BUT THE MED CENTER NEEDED MY POWER CELL. IT WAS THE ONLY WAY.
HAHAHAHAHA!
MAYBE NEXT TIME.

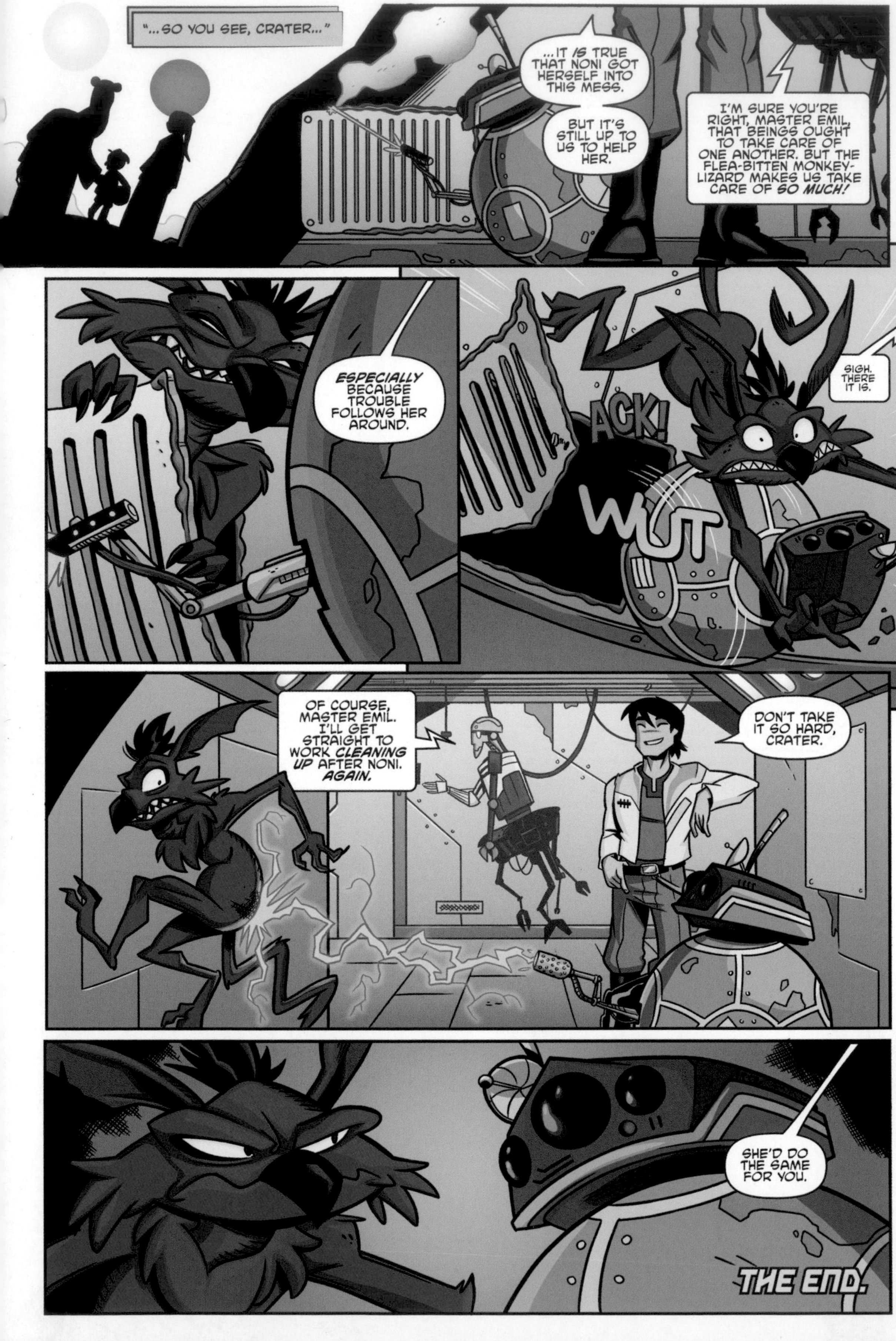
"...SO YOU SEE, CRATER..."
...IT IS TRUE THAT NONI GOT HERSELF INTO THIS MESS.
BUT IT'S STILL UP TO US TO HELP HER.
I'M SURE YOU'RE RIGHT, MASTER EMIL, THAT BEINGS OUGHT TO TAKE CARE OF ONE ANOTHER. BUT THE FLEA-BITTEN MONKEY-LIZARD MAKES US TAKE CARE OF SO MUCH!
ESPECIALLY BECAUSE TROUBLE FOLLOWS HER AROUND.
ACK!
WUT
SIGH. THERE IT IS.
OF COURSE, MASTER EMIL. I'LL GET STRAIGHT TO WORK CLEANING UP AFTER NONI. AGAIN.
DON'T TAKE IT SO HARD, CRATER.
SHE'D DO THE SAME FOR YOU.
THE END.

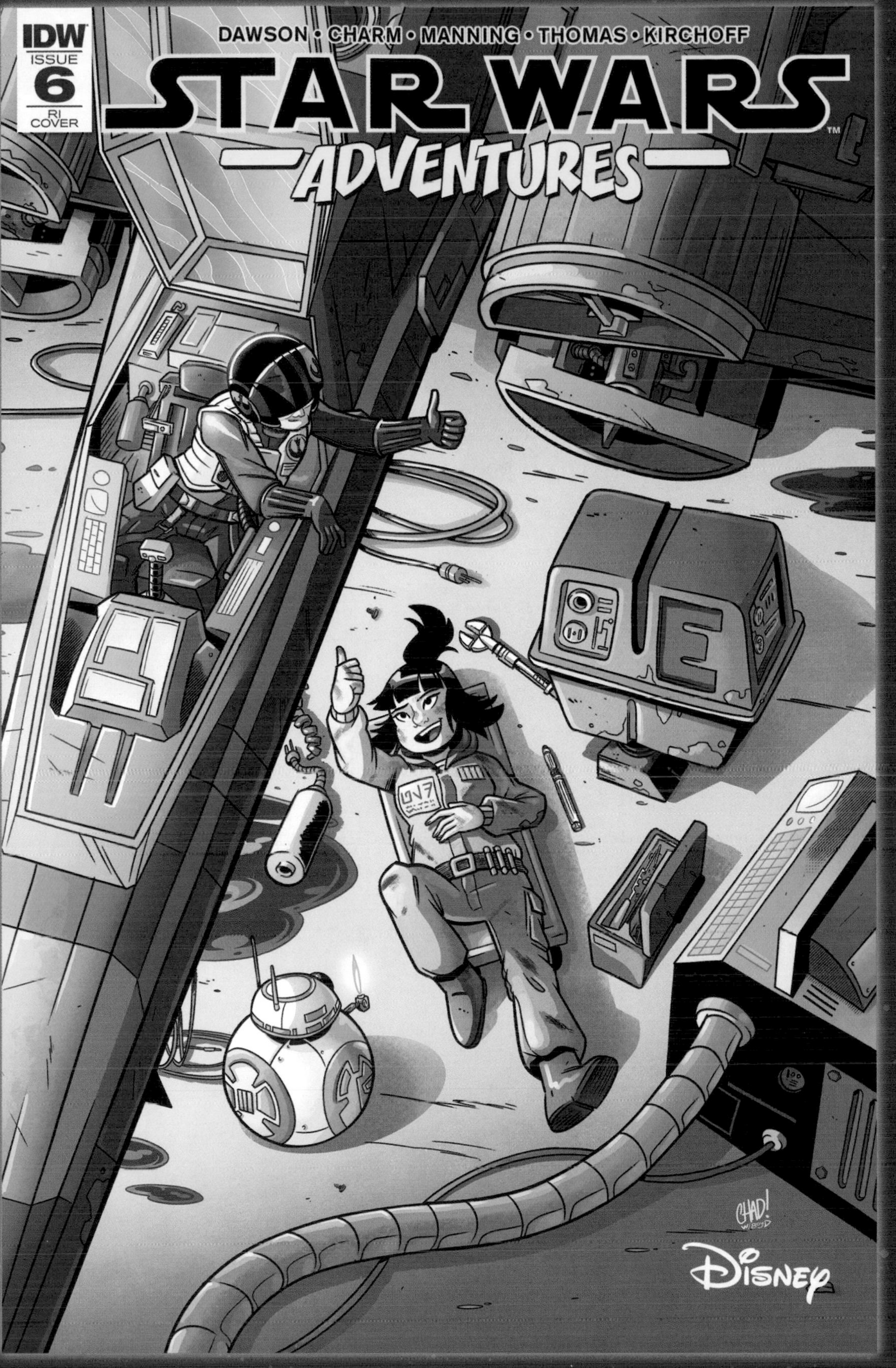
IDW
ISSUE
6
RI
COVER
DAWSON • CHARM • MANNING • THOMAS • KIRCHOFF
STAR WARS
ADVENTURES
Disney

Star Wars Adventures #6
Variant cover RI artwork by Chad Thomas

STAR WARS ADVENTURES

COLLECT THEM ALL!

Set of 6 Hardcover Books ISBN: 978-1-5321-4284-0

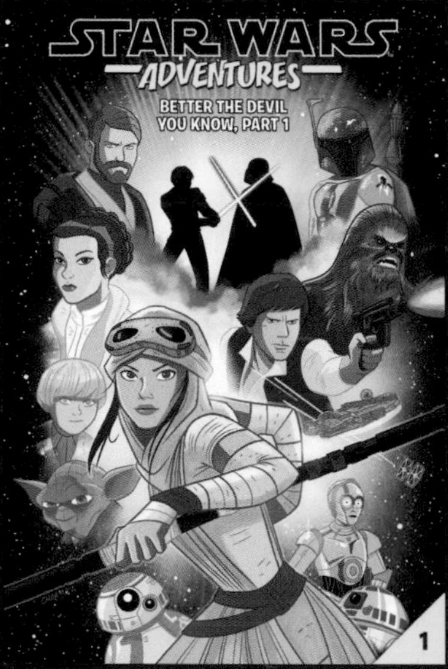
STAR WARS
ADVENTURES
BETTER THE DEVIL YOU KNOW, PART 1
1

**Hardcover Book ISBN
978-1-5321-4285-7**

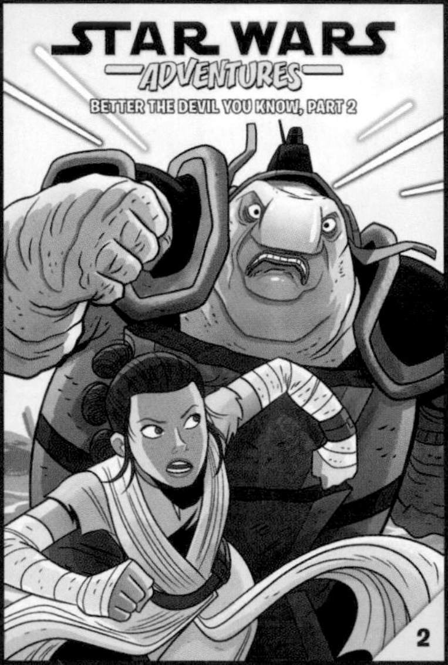
STAR WARS
ADVENTURES
BETTER THE DEVIL YOU KNOW, PART 2
2

**Hardcover Book ISBN
978-1-5321-4286-4**

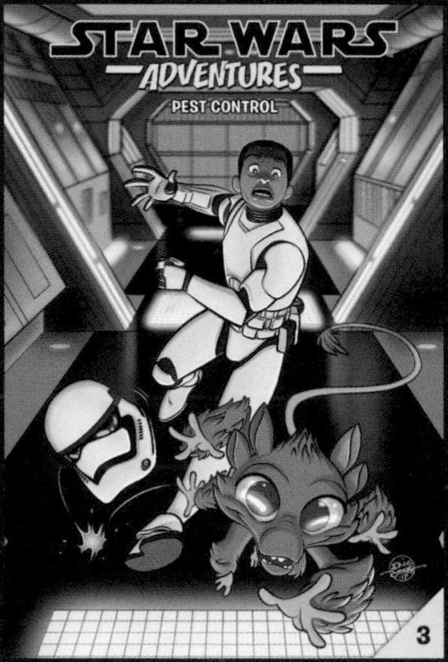
STAR WARS
ADVENTURES
PEST CONTROL
3

**Hardcover Book ISBN
978-1-5321-4287-1**

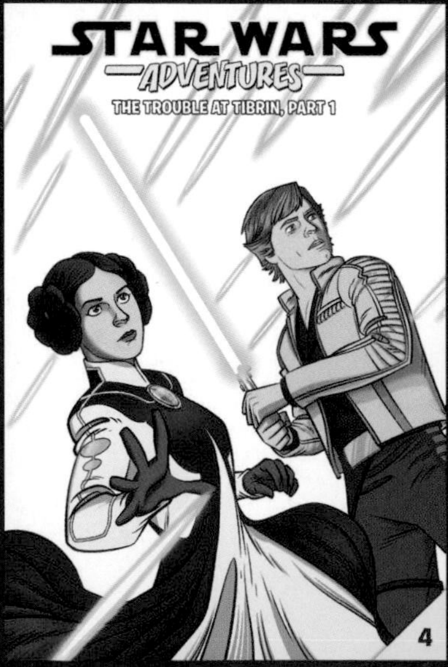
STAR WARS
ADVENTURES
THE TROUBLE AT TIBRIN, PART 1
4

**Hardcover Book ISBN
978-1-5321-4288-8**

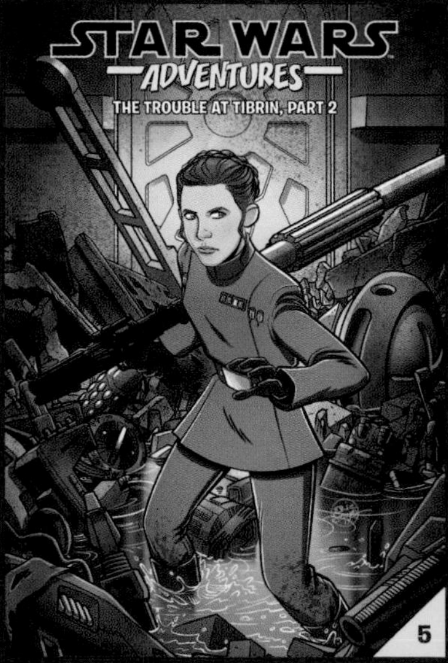
STAR WARS
ADVENTURES
THE TROUBLE AT TIBRIN, PART 2
5

**Hardcover Book ISBN
978-1-5321-4289-5**

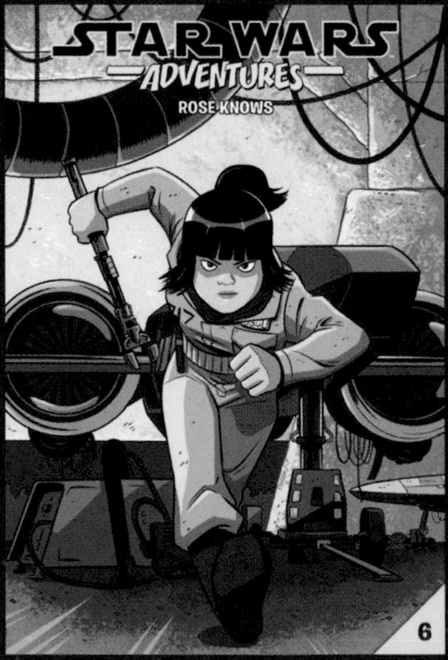
STAR WARS
ADVENTURES
ROSE KNOWS
6

**Hardcover Book ISBN
978-1-5321-4290-1**